The trouble begins. . . .

"I MUST BE SEEING THINGS, JON, BUT IT looked like you just floated."

Jon felt panic. He hadn't directed his body to levitate.

"I kind of skipped," he replied to his father. What had happened? Could his levitation get out of control?

Jon reminded himself to be more careful in the future. The floating had surprised him as much as it had surprised his father. Maybe his brain was having so much fun with levitation that it was taking control. That was a scary thought.

He had no intention of stopping this wonderful, miraculous, sensational, extraordinary, supernatural use of his brain cells. But at the same time, he had to be able to control them.

The Boy
Who Could Fly
Without a Motor

The Boy
Who Could Fly
Without a Motor

~

THEODORE TAYLOR

HARCOURT, INC.

Orlando   Austin   New York

San Diego   Toronto   London

www.HarcourtBooks.com

First Harcourt paperback edition 2004

The Library of Congress has cataloged
the hardcover edition as follows:
Taylor, Theodore, 1921–
The boy who could fly without a motor/by Theodore Taylor.
p. cm.
Summary: In 1935, living at a lighthouse near San Francisco,
a lonely nine-year-old boy inadvertently summons
a magician who teaches him the secret of flying.
[1. Flight—Fiction.   2. Magicians—Fiction.
3. Loneliness—Fiction.]   I. Title.
PZ7.T2186Br   2002
[Fic]—dc21   2001039848
ISBN 0-15-216529-0   ISBN 0-15-204767-0 pb

Text set in Bembo
Display set in Nicolas Cochin
Designed by Cathy Riggs

A C E G H F D B

Printed in the United States of America

For great-grandsons Adam and Nathaniel,
with much love
—T. T.

~ ONE ~

A MERE FIFTY-TWO POUNDS, FOUR-FEET-
two-inches tall, brown eyed and brown
haired, nine-year-old Jonathan Jeffers
thought he was the loneliest boy on Earth.

He lived with his father, James, and his
mother, Mabel, in a red-painted cottage
on Clementine Rock, near Three Fathom
Shoal and Persiphone Reef, next to an old
white-painted brick lighthouse, nineteen
miles off the coast of California.

He had a big brown-and-black dog
named Smacks, a dog of many breeds.
They were constant companions, as Jon

desperately needed a friend. Smacks served him as best he could just by being there.

All night and on foggy days, the strong beam of the lighthouse went around and around, warning ships to stay away from the rock, the shoal, and the reef. The light was powered by a big generator, and Jon's father, a boatswain mate first class in the United States Coast Guard—or bosun— was the keeper. On a clear night, the light could be seen from passing ships twenty-two miles away.

When the heavy, cold mists rolled in toward San Francisco, which was to the north of Clementine, the hoarse foghorn also bellowed. Hour after hour. Sometimes day after day. AHHHHHH-RURH-RRRR-AAAA- AAAATS.

It sounded like "Ah, rats" to Jon, who had a strong oval face and an imagination as broad as the sweep of the light.

He hated the fog and the "Ah, rats" horn. And he didn't exactly like the seals that barked most of the day on the outlying rocks, either.

On the nights when the eaves were dripping and the horn was blowing, Jon sometimes thought of the famous Ghosts of Clementine. The rock was named after the sailing ship that had crashed into it in 1850. The ship had been bound for San Francisco, carrying Chinese workers from Canton to build railroads.

All of the 129 men had died, and their ghosts were still around the rock, or so Jon had been told by an older girl, Eunice

Jones, the daughter in the Coast Guard family the Jeffers had replaced. Eunice was thirteen, tall for her age, and skinny as spaghetti. She knew the rock's history. She'd said that when the gray fog blanket was thick, the ghosts rose out of the sea and climbed up the steep sides of Clementine, which was shaped like a long high box with coarse grass on top. The sodden ghosts moaned in sorrow as they climbed. Jon had had some horrendous dreams as the result of Eunice's stories and that deep-throated foghorn.

Eunice had said she'd met some of the "living-dead" ghosts herself and that Jon would likely meet a few as well. They were spooky but pitiful and harmless, and they lived under the rock, she'd said. Jon had thought Eunice was a little spooky herself. She had long fingers and lisped.

There also were ghosts of shipwrecked sailors out at Three Fathom Shoal and Persiphone Reef, Eunice had told him. The rusted prow of a steel ship still rode the reef, sticking up like an open shark's jaw, water washing over it. Altogether more than three hundred people had died on the rock, the shoal, and the reef before the government had erected the lighthouse sixty years ago.

Jon's mother and father said that the ghosts were utter nonsense. Ghosts do not exist, they said. Ghosts do not swim, they said. And they do not live under the rock.

Jon tried to believe them, but on some nights, when the horn went silent for its programmed thirty seconds, Jon thought he heard the ghosts moaning and was afraid to peer out his window into the rolls of thick mist. Perhaps a dripping, pitiful Chinese face would be there, staring in at him. Even Smacks seemed nervous on these occasions.

His father said, "Jon, don't let your imagination hear sounds that aren't there."

But Jon's problem was his *ears,* not his imagination. His hearing was too sharp and the sounds seemed too real, so he wrapped his head with his pillow those nights and shivered, hoping the ghosts wouldn't come in.

Eunice had said he would go crazy out there.

Maybe he *would* go crazy. His father

had to serve three years on the rock. One year had gone by so far.

Jon did have things to keep him occupied. He'd gone through primary school in San Francisco, and now his mother taught him five mornings a week, with textbooks and exams from the mainland. They also had a radio, and after he listened to the many programs, Jon had dreams that carried him around the globe. New York, London, Tokyo, Paris. Anywhere but Clementine. *Anywhere!*

To amuse himself during his free daylight hours, Jon kept an eye out for big ships passing Clementine Light. He'd run up to the tower, Smacks at his heels, and watch them through his father's powerful telescope. If they came close enough, Jon would wave and record their names in his logbook. Anything to entertain himself. Anything to stay busy.

In good weather, private planes on Sunday joyrides would come out from shore and circle the lighthouse. Jon would again run to the light platform and wave. The pilots would often wave back. The open-cockpit biplanes were his favorite. Jon also built model airplanes, mostly World War I fighters, to pass the time and take his mind off the Clementine ghosts.

~ TWO ~

LAST YEAR JON'S GRANDPARENTS IN NEW Mexico had given him a subscription to *Popular Science* magazine, and he read every issue cover to cover. Calling himself Mr. J. Jeffers, he'd written to various advertisers about mail courses for bodybuilding, being a detective, and careers in aviation and electronics.

It was 1935, and a time of great scientific advancements. Charles Lindbergh had flown alone across the Atlantic, radio and talking pictures had been invented, and the first liquid-fueled rocket had been launched. Jon made notes about all these amazing events. He'd even written to Lindbergh, asking him to be a pen pal, but he hadn't yet heard back.

There was one particular article in an issue of *Popular Science* that Jon kept reading and rereading. Written by a doctor of parapsychology, someone who deals in psychic phenomena, it was about telepathy, or sending and receiving messages using nothing more than the mind. Hoping to cure his loneliness, Jon began to practice telepathy, sending messages all over the place, sometimes concentrating so hard he got headaches. But, so far, he'd never received a mental-wave message back from any listener. Perhaps he was too young, he thought, and his brain wasn't developed enough.

Before becoming involved in telepathy, Jon had stuffed messages into bottles, giving his exact latitude and longitude, and cast them into the ocean: *Help! Help! I am shipwrecked and stranded on a terrible rock that is full of ghosts.* Signed: *Jon Jeffers, Seaman First Class. U.S. Coast Guard*

He'd also make up stories and tell them to his parents during supper, stories like "Albie, the Albatross," about how Jonathan Jeffers rode the back of a big bird to Paris, or "In the Ice," in which he and Smacks were adrift on an ice floe in the Arctic Ocean. He told stories about cowboys and pirates and bandits. They weren't long, but they were stories with a definite beginning, middle, and end.

"Someday you'll be a writer," his mother said proudly.

But at the moment, Jon was only interested in getting off Clementine Rock. His problem was very simple: Except for Smacks he had no playmates, no friends, and no one to talk to except his mother and father and the seals and seabirds surrounding Clementine.

The best time on the island was when the Coast Guard supply boat came to the rock. Even Smacks would bark joyfully as the boat approached. It steamed out twice a month, weather permitting, with fresh vegetables, milk, meat, mail, and back issues of the *San Francisco Chronicle*.

The Coast Guard crew usually brought Jon candy and a book or two when they came, but when the tug pulled away from the small dock at the base of the rock, bound back to San Francisco, Jon always felt the same old sadness.

Once a year, thankfully, the Jeffers family had shore leave—sixty days on the mainland. On their first trip, they visited relatives, went to movies and amusement parks, shopped for clothes, and ate at restaurants. It was a heavenly time.

But all too soon they were sent straight back to the rock, where the wind softly ruffled the thick grass outside their cottage or sometimes roared, flattening the grass and driving sheets of cold rain before it.

Jon was back to talking to Smacks and the wheeling birds, fishing off the dock, or watching the passing ships through his father's telescope, wishing he were aboard them. Back to the same awful life on

Clementine that Eunice had warned him about, and after he did all these things, there was nothing left to do except think and dream, listen to the radio, and practice telepathy.

On clear nights he'd often look out of his window at the far-off glow of the city, wishing he were there. He thought it would be wonderful to walk on water, to set off across the waves and visit San Francisco. But it would be a long hike. One afternoon he decided it would be much better to tread on air and arrive in the big city without wet feet. *Fly over! Escape the rock! What a terrific idea!*

He talked to Smacks about it, maybe a loony thing to do. But anything he did was okay with Smacks.

So, during the next few days, Jon

thought a lot about body flying. He told his mother, and she said it was quite natural to think about flying through the air, looking down on Earth. She remembered a dream she'd had in childhood, when she'd flown without flapping her arms. She agreed it would be glorious to actually body fly.

On some nights, in his small bed with its four red posts and the yellow spread on which his mother had embroidered a pelican, Jon would imagine that the bed had mystical powers and could fly out the wide window, over his mother's pots of geraniums. In one dream, he saw himself sitting on the four-poster as it zipped over the waves and then landed in the heart of the city, causing a great commotion.

Once, he actually got out of bed and

measured the window. By tilting the bed just a little, he would be able to pass through with ease.

On these nights he also practiced telepathy: *Hello, out there. This is Jon Jeffers, wanting to talk to someone about being stranded on a rock in the Pacific Ocean. I need advice on how to body fly.*

Somewhere someone had to be listening.

~ THREE ~

ON AN UNUSUALLY SUNNY AND ALMOST warm morning in September, after a windy night with the seas crashing against Clementine Rock, Jon walked down the winding path to the tiny beach cove. He wanted to see if anything had washed up during the night. Smacks trotted behind him, down the fifty-four steps to the water.

Occasionally, Jon would find a glass fishing-net float from Japan or a wooden box with foreign lettering or a bottle or a life ring. Once, an airplane wing tank washed ashore and Jon's father cut a big hole in it. The tank became a fine swing, up by the red cottage.

The tide was far out that morning, and Jon poked around the damp, rippled sand with his toes, seeing nothing of interest aside from some empty clam and spiral shells. The sunning seals, which shared their rocks with the fish-diving pelicans and cormorants, were strangely quiet, as if something or someone had cast a spell over the cove. Never had they been so silent. They almost seemed frightened.

Suddenly, Jon saw *him*. There, sitting on a rock mound to the far side of the cove, was a strange man in a strange cos-tume. A split down the front of his red satin gown revealed pants of the blackest velvet and shoes of red fur that curled up at the toes. His white hair was swept back from his forehead and fell in a braid almost to the middle of his back. On top of his head perched a small black hat that looked like an overturned cup.

Smacks saw him, too. He always barked at anything that invaded Clementine, even the occasional schools of killer whales that steered too close to the rock. But this time Smacks didn't bark. He stared at the stranger and then turned and ran back up the fifty-four steps, tail between his legs.

The visitor was as fat as Jon's father was skinny. His face was as round as a pumpkin and as unusual as this unusual day. His skin was orange brown and looked as though a glistening layer of grease had been spread all over it. He appeared to be very old, yet he had no wrinkles. Over his button nose, the visitor stared out toward Three Fathom Shoal. Was he a friend of Eunice Jones?

Jon considered running up the path to summon his father, who was painting high on the lighthouse's outer steps. His mother was probably still inside. Jon was certain they'd both like to meet this man. Or would they? Yet Jon thought he might be seeing something that wasn't there at all. Wasn't there at all. Maybe he was dreaming in his four-poster while still wide awake? Or maybe he was just going crazy, like Eunice had predicted.

Jon was startled but somehow not

frightened. Perhaps the visitor had indeed cast a spell over the entire cove. The seals had shut up and so had Smacks. The gulls had vanished. And where was the man's boat? He wasn't wet, so he couldn't have swum in. Jon thought again of Eunice and the Ghosts of Clementine. But this old man looked nothing like the ghosts she had described as clad in spiderwebs, with white gelatin eyes and clammy hands.

Not wanting to say the first word but wanting to attract attention, Jon picked up a small piece of driftwood and threw it into the water. The stranger quickly turned his head.

"Good morning," the man said pleasantly, in English. He spoke with a soft accent that Jon had never heard on the mainland or over the radio. It was clearly a foreign voice.

"I live up there," said Jon, pointing back over his own shoulder. Why wasn't he frightened?

"I know."

"How could you know?" It was a sensible question for Jon to ask.

"I saw you come down the path."

"But you weren't even here."

"Yes, I was," the man said, matter-of-factly.

"Are you dead? Are you a ghost?"

"Yes, I'm long dead, but I refuse to be a silly ghost. I died when the Clementine crashed into this foul chunk of what was once a volcano. I'd been sent by the Manchu dynasty to entertain my fellow countrymen in that idiotic San Francisco. Don't ask me more stupid questions, Jon."

"How do you know my name?"

The man laughed a lemon laugh, slightly sour. "I've been getting your foolish vibrations for months."

"My 'vibrations'?" The telepathy had worked!

"Your thoughts and your dreams, dear boy. You've pestered me night after night as I've voyaged around, not knowing you'd picked me as your target. I kept receiving *body flying, body flying,* over and over and over. I've found it quite difficult to concentrate on more important things. And now that I've met you, I see you're most insignificant, not worthy of concentration."

Jon didn't know what to say. He kept looking into the man's eyes. They seemed endless. Two green tunnels that went on forever. *How did he get here? Where did he come from?*

"By the way," the visitor announced, "I'm the Great Ling Wu, magician and member of the Celestial Court, and I've come here to get you to leave me alone."

~ FOUR ~

"I DON'T KNOW WHAT THE CELESTIAL
Court is," said Jon Jeffers.

"Heathen! If you had a thimbleful of
brains, you'd know I am heavenly royalty,
entertainer of emperors, a son of Buddha."

Jon also did not know what *heathen*
meant, much less those other things.

Reading his mind, Ling Wu sighed and
said, "A heathen is an unworthy one, a
useless one; one who is not born in the
light of Buddha. *That is you.*"

Jon swallowed and thought again about

running up the path for his father, to prove he wasn't dreaming. And to prove he wasn't insane.

But his feet seemed firmly glued into the sand. He couldn't even wiggle his toes. To change the subject from how useless he was, Jon said, "I've never seen clothes like yours."

"Is there something wrong with my clothes?" Ling Wu snorted.

"I've just never seen a man in a red gown. Or velvet pants."

"Should I appear in beggars' rags?" Ling Wu stormed.

"If you live with the other ghosts, why aren't your clothes wet?" That was a legitimate question, Jon thought.

"You are an impudent boy and don't

deserve answers of any kind," said Ling Wu.

Not knowing what to say or how to please this ghost who wasn't a ghost, Jon apologized.

"Do you know what I can do?" asked the Great Ling Wu.

"No, sir."

The roly-poly man extended sausage-like fingers that were studded with rings in which huge, spinning red stones were set.

Before Jon could blink, a white dove appeared on one of the fingers and then fluttered off into the air. Suddenly, a black rabbit hung by its ears from Ling Wu's left hand. When Ling Wu released it, it bounded up the path, finally vanishing just like the dove, and Ling Wu flicked a speck of dust from the rich red cloth of his gown as though he'd done nothing at all.

Jon felt like saying "They weren't real" but didn't dare. Ling Wu might make him vanish, too.

"I am the greatest magician ever, but much more than that, much more," intoned Ling Wu, without the slightest modesty. "No one dead a thousand years, and twice again, or living ten thousand years from now, will ever astound and amaze as I have astounded and amazed."

The green eyes glittered and the parchment skin glistened.

"Show me another trick, please," Jon said.

"*Trick?*" roared Ling Wu. "Trick?"

Jon knew he'd said the wrong word.

"I've performed my art for emperors and empresses in imperial palaces and the great halls and fairs of Peking. Trick indeed, ant brain!"

Jon nodded, feeling smaller and more insignificant than any ant on earth.

Ling Wu's eyes narrowed, his smooth skin drawing tight around them. "Watch closely."

Before Jon's eyes, across the incoming tide, the Great Ling Wu was rising as if invisible strings tugged him toward heaven. His body was soon one foot, two feet, three feet, off the brown pebbly rock. Lying back, enjoying himself, he extended his legs and laughed smugly.

"You're floating," Jon said breathlessly.

"Clearly," replied Ling Wu.

Jon looked toward the lighthouse and the figure of his father far up the iron ladder. He opened his mouth to shout so that his father could see this marvelous feat that was happening down in their cove.

"Uh-uh," warned Ling Wu. "This is for your eyes only. You are *never* to mention this as long as you live. If you do, I'll turn you into a one-eyed calico toad."

Jon clamped his lips together.

The magician turned one way and another. He flapped the sleeves of his gown as if he were a bird, then kicked as if swimming in thin air was as easy as swimming in water.

He turned his head and an almost evil smile crossed his face.

Jon gasped. Ling Wu wasn't just floating. He was body flying.

~ FIVE ~

"I CAN'T BELIEVE IT," SAID JON, WATCH-
ing the Chinese magician float comfort-
ably in the air, a fat stringless kite, a
multicolored bird.

"But you do see it, don't you?" asked
Ling Wu, finally lowering himself to the
rock, adjusting his magnificent red gown
as he sat down again.

"Is it the robe? Is that how you do it?"
Jon asked excitedly.

"Not at all."

"Well, how do you do it?"

"Do what?"

"Body fly."

"Levitation, my child."

"Levi?..."

"Tation. *L-e-v-i-t-a-t-i-o-n.*"

It was a huge, teeth-pulling, tongue-wrapping word. *Levitation!*

"Anyone can do anything, provided they know how."

Jon's voice was as thick as cream when he asked, "Can I?"

Ling Wu's green eyes sharpened until they were stabbing green points afire with anger. "You're asking me for my secrets! I knew you would, unworthy heathen!"

There was that awful word again. "Only this one secret," Jon somehow found the courage to say. He could leave Clementine now and then, find friends on the mainland, have fun, then fly home. "Only one, sir."

"Only this one secret, you earthworm. You say it so lightly. The very idea. Of all the nerve." Ling Wu was again livid with rage. His skin had turned as crimson as his gown. His jowls quivered and his thick fingers shook.

Jon had never been so terrified in his entire life, knowing Ling Wu could easily make him vanish like the dove and the rabbit. The green points of Ling Wu's eyes raked him, searched his insides, and went straight into his thudding heart.

Yet he found the courage to speak again. "Please! You don't know how lonely my life has been. Some mornings I don't even want to wake up."

Ling Wu turned off his rage as if it were faucet water. "Hmh. You're forgiven for being so greedy, I suppose." Then a fat finger aimed toward Jon's chest. "You'll promise to tell no one. Ever? Even after death? We've never met! I don't exist!"

"No one, I promise."

"Not your honorable father?"

"Not my honorable father."

"Not your honorable mother?"

"Not my honorable mother."

"Or honorable aunt or uncle or cousin or friend or foe?..."

Jon's mouth was as dry as uncooked oatmeal. He began to repeat, "'Or honorable aunt or uncle—'"

"Never mind," Ling Wu broke in sharply. "No one shall you ever tell. Ever. Ever and ever. I don't exist."

"No one shall I ever tell. Ever. Ever and ever. You don't exist." The promise was to last until death did him part—and beyond. Never would he tell.

The magician's green eyes were now squinting and glinting. "On threat of being boiled in dragon's bile and having flaming straw stuffed up your nose..." His hand shot out, grasping a bundle of flaming straw. He tossed it into the air.

Jon could hardly breathe.

"...your ears turned into goat's horns and your toes nailed to a shark's back..." Ling Wu nodded toward the cove. A ten-foot shark suddenly patrolled it.

Feeling faint, Jon managed to reply weakly, "No one shall I ever tell—"

"On absolute oath to a member of the Celestial Court who has done the Three Kneelings and Nine Knockings..."

Jon repeated in a bare whisper, "'On oath to—'"

"Never mind," said Ling Wu.

He folded his arms over his potbelly and stared at Jon Jeffers for quite a while, then took a deep breath. "All right, then. I shall tell you."

SIX

"WITH MY AMAZING, ASTOUNDING brain I levitate. That's all," said Ling Wu. "My own astonishing brain."

"Like you," the magician went on, "I have billions of brain cells. But unlike you, and most other unworthy people, I use them. I levitate with maybe five hundred million. I could do it with less, but I feel more comfortable with that many holding me up."

With a tummy the size of a washtub, Ling Wu likely *needed* five hundred million cells, Jon thought. He'd read that every human had billions of brain cells.

But how did one command one's brain cells to levitate? Jon did not dare ask.

"Concentration, my unworthy," Ling Wu continued. "I put all that amazing and astounding energy together. It's very powerful, believe me. Using seven hundred million cells, I can lift that boat over there."

Jon watched as his father's dory, chained to a ring embedded in the rock, rose up as if a giant blast of air were beneath it. Straining against the chain for a minute or so, it settled again.

With glee, his almost evil eyes again laughing, Ling Wu then said, "If I used a billion cells, I could lift that lighthouse."

"Oh, please don't!" Jon cried out, fearing his father would tumble off the side.

"Hmh," said Ling Wu thoughtfully, scanning the tall white cylinder.

Jon desperately wanted to change the subject. He did not doubt that the magician could raise the old brick tower. He said, "All I have to do is concentrate, then I can levi..."

"Tate!" Ling Wu nodded, shifting his eyes from the lighthouse. "Concentrate and levitate."

"Just tell myself I can do it, over and over," Jon said excitedly.

"Exactly."

Jon closed his eyes on the very spot and began to concentrate.

"Idiot heathen," Ling Wu lashed out,

and Jon opened his eyes. "You cannot learn overnight. Your body has to get used to the idea. It may take weeks."

"I'll practice," Jon said eagerly.

Ling Wu nodded again. "You must practice many, many times. And once you learn how, don't do foolish things. Do it where no one will see you. People aren't used to seeing other people levitating all over the place. Do it at night."

But Jon wasn't really listening. He was thinking about what fun it would be for people to see him floating and flying. Here, there, and everywhere, like a butterfly, a hummingbird.

Ling Wu, however, seemed to know that Jon was apt to get into terrible trouble, and as if immediately regretting having revealed his secret, he said, "People who don't listen to warnings are likely to find disaster. Do not fly in fog or thunderstorms or high winds. And *don't* fly long distances—especially at first."

Jon nodded, but the words might just as well have been tossed into the ocean breeze. His thoughts were consumed by that magic word—*levitation.*

Ling Wu shrugged. "Have fun, Jon Jeffers. Now you will actually be able to fly like a hawk or a heron or a hummingbird. You will soar like a kite. But do not forget that a kite must have a string to hold it to the earth. You will not have one."

But Jon was not thinking of kite strings. He was thinking of darting along on high—over cities and highways, over

beaches and streets, forests and rivers—
waving to everyone below: *Hello down
there; I'm Jon Jeffers!* Ling Wu was right—
he'd never be lonely again.

But then he heard Ling Wu's sharp,
"Turn around, unworthy."

Obediently, he turned, looking up toward the top of the lighthouse, where his
father was still painting. Then Jon thought
he heard the sound of far-off temple bells.
When he turned back, the Great Ling Wu
was gone. The seals began to bark again.

Smacks, realizing the visitor had departed, left his hiding place and bravely
raced down the fifty-four steps, matching
the seals' hoarse bleats and honks.

Jon said to him, "Coward! I just
learned how to fly."

Ling Wu had not included best-friend dogs in his orders never to tell anyone about concentrating and levitating, or that he even existed.

Jon realized he could now move his feet in the sand again and took a few steps back to the dock. He looked all around the cove. He went over to the dory. There was no sign that it had been lifted. He went to the pebbly rock where the magician had sat. Not even a trace of Ling Wu's gown and velvet pants, not a stray thread. Was Ling Wu a living ghost? Was it all a silly daydream? Or was he going insane, as Eunice had predicted?

For a moment Jon thought about telling his mother and father what had happened. But then he had a vision of being boiled in dragon's bile, whatever that was, along with having his toes nailed to a shark's back and flaming straw stuffed up his nose.

Best keep it all to himself.

~ SEVEN ~

THAT NIGHT AT SUPPER, OVER BEEF STEW and homemade noodles, his favorite meal, Jon decided to ask his father a question. The question wouldn't give away Ling Wu's secret but might help prove Jon wasn't just daydreaming in the cove. "What, exactly, does *levitation* mean?"

Frowning a bit, his father answered, "It means 'to rise up, to float in the air'..."

His mother added, "Doesn't happen, Jon. It means 'overcoming gravity.' It's supernatural. Where did you hear the word?"

"The Moonbeam Show." A lie. Then, "Mom, what is gravity?"

"It is the force of attraction by which terrestrial bodies tend to fall toward the center of the earth." She was so smart. She'd once been a teacher.

Jon frowned helplessly. What were terrestrial bodies?

She said, "Tomorrow morning we'll go deeper into that. Eat your supper."

He ate a few more bites, then said to both of them, "What is dragon's bile?"

His father laughed. "I guess it's the acid in a dragon's stomach."

His mother said, "Dragon's bile, *ugh*. I should be paying more attention to the shows you listen to."

Jon had his own radio set. He smiled

faintly at them. "What is the Celestial Court?"

"It's a heavenly court," said his mother.

He was now certain that Ling Wu had indeed visited Clementine Cove; perhaps Eunice was right and Ling Wu lived in a sea cavern beneath the rock with the other ghosts without getting wet. Or maybe he lived in China. Oh, what his parents *didn't* know. He was pretty sure they'd never talked to a living-dead magician.

"You're asking unusual questions tonight, Jon. But I suppose that's how you get an education," his mother said.

Jon half smiled, anxious to leave the table. Hurriedly finishing the bowl of stew and noodles as his parents began to talk about other things, Jon said, "I think I'll go to bed."

His mother looked over with alarm. He usually fought to stay up late. "Do you feel all right?"

"I'm just sleepy."

So, Jon kissed them both and ran off to his room, Smacks at his heels. He quickly undressed, said his prayers, climbed into bed, then took the deepest breath he could.

It was time to experiment.

Pushing the pillow away so his body would be flat, he began to whisper, "Rise, Jon, rise! Rise, Jon, rise..." *Go to work, brain cells,* he thought.

Smacks cocked his head one way, then the other. He was accustomed to his human friend talking to himself.

The setting was right, Jon thought. A beam of moonlight put a wand through his window. There was no fog, and no ghosts were climbing the cliffs.

He repeated himself again and again, expecting that at any moment he'd feel himself levitating.

Smacks looked and listened for a while, then went to sleep.

Nothing happened. Jon thought that maybe the covers were holding him down. He kicked them off and concentrated once more. Not a fraction of an inch did he move.

Trying to remember exactly what the Great Ling Wu had said, he started all over again, hoping he could gather five hundred million cells into one space in his head, and let them work collectively to raise him up.

"Five hundred million cells, lift me. I order you to lift me!"

That didn't work, either.

So, he went back to repeating, "Rise, Jon, rise." He finally fell asleep while saying it.

At about nine-thirty his mother came into the room and saw that the covers were pushed to the end of the bed. She felt his forehead. No fever. She tucked him in and left the room.

Smacks sighed and went back to sleep. It had been a trying day.

EIGHT

ALL THE NEXT DAY JON PRACTICED.

He practiced down on the pebbly rock where Ling Wu had sat, and up in the coarse grass. He climbed to the top of the lighthouse, to the small walkway outside the lantern room. Smacks followed him, as usual. He was lonesome, too.

Believing it might help to be up that high, 160 feet off the ground, Jon lay down on the steel decking and began to repeat, "Rise, Jon, rise!" Nothing rose except the updrafts of wind.

By this time his brain was so tired from all the effort, Jon gave up and went slowly down the spiraling ladder to the inside steps.

At twilight Jon was still exhausted and so went straight to bed after supper. He fell asleep within a few minutes, not thinking once about Ling Wu or levitation. He slept for seven hours straight but awoke suddenly at 2:00 A.M. He no longer felt tired. His brain was rested, too. He looked around. Every ten seconds the beam of bright light filled his window, and then blackness briefly returned. The wind drummed at the red cottage, and he could hear the surf pounding and sloshing at the base of the rock.

It would be a good time to try again, he thought.

For a moment he lay very still and then pushed the covers down. Breathing slowly, and relaxing, he concentrated. In a small voice inside his head, he directed five hundred million brain cells to lift him. He did not say it aloud this time.

Silently, he commanded, *Rise, Jon, rise.* Then he felt something happening.

Impossibly, incredibly, wondrously, he was lifting up from the sheet. An inch, then another, then another. He was afraid to move a muscle or take a breath. He only moved his eyes. Right and left and down, focusing on his toes.

Was he imagining this? Or was it happening? He was tempted to take one hand and feel beneath his back to make certain he was suspended in air. *No,* he thought. *I'll just stay here a moment and float; be very still.* If the spell had caught him—if it was true levitation—he didn't want to ruin it. *If only Ling Wu could see me now.*

Then he remembered the large mirror on top of his dresser. From the bed he could always look into it. Sometimes on awakening, he even made faces into it.

He looked to the right and waited for the next beam of light to flash by the window. The seconds ticked off, and then in a bright explosion he saw a brown-eyed, brown-haired boy of nine named Jonathan Jeffers floating in the air above his own bed.

He also saw Smacks—with owl eyes, getting ready to sound alarm at his master's strange and dangerous position—and whispered urgently, "Don't bark; you'll ruin everything."

Was there ever a human on earth, old or young or skinny or fat, who hadn't thought about this, dreamed of it? Pumping along on an aerial road that wasn't there. Taking a nap on a cloud. Waving to an eagle. Dancing over rooftops.

Peter Pan had done it!

That Arabian on his carpet had done it!

Ling Wu had done it!

And now Jon Jeffers had done it!

It was impossibly, incredibly wondrous. Jon felt like shouting, screaming, and whooping but didn't dare. Thinking he was having a nightmare, his parents would come rushing in. They'd both faint upon seeing their only son in the midst of levitation. Then they'd ask questions.

Jon took a deep breath and said aloud, "That way." Nothing happened.

So, he focused his mind, harnessed all his cells, and said it silently. Suddenly, he was turning, going straight into the mirror, which fell with a loud bang as Jon bounced off, crying out with pain.

Luckily, he had de-levitated before his parents came running into the room, to find him sprawled on top of the dresser.

"What in the world is going on?" his father shouted, eyes heavy with sleep.

"I must have had a bad dream," said Jon. Another white lie.

"You certainly did," said his mother. "Are you hurt?"

"No," Jon said, but his head throbbed.

"How did you get on top of the dresser?" she asked.

"I don't know," Jon replied, telling his fourth lie in two days.

⁓ NINE ⁓

THE NEXT DAY, AFTER HIS LESSONS, JON stretched out on the cove sand and practiced levitating. Sometimes he rose several inches above the ground, but he didn't dare try to move around. Mostly he did a lot of thinking. He knew he'd have to learn to time himself and to turn at the proper minute or else he'd crash into things.

Once, his father came halfway down the path and shouted, "What are you doing, Jon?"

"Oh, nothing," Jon answered.

Another time his mother came down and almost caught him afloat. He was two inches off the sand when she called, "Lunch!"

He descended in a hurry, thinking it was a good thing she hadn't sneaked up on him. How would he explain without telling his parents about Ling Wu and risking having his toes nailed to a shark's back?

The trouble with Clementine was that there was no place to experiment with body flying aside from in his room. Most every square foot of the cove could be seen from the bluff, and the top of the dock was as open as a prairie.

That night Jon listened to the radio with his parents, but his mind wasn't on the Grand Ole Opry. He could think only of getting to his room and on top of his bed. Or on the floor, or anywhere. Maybe he didn't even have to lie down. Maybe he could levitate while he was on his feet. Jon couldn't wait to try. Finally, at eight-thirty, he said good night to his parents, put on his pajamas, said his prayers, and got into bed.

He tossed restlessly for an hour, until he heard his father's snores. His mother usually fell asleep first, so Jon figured they were both settled for the night.

Jon concentrated and slowly rose. Timing his turns, he carefully moved himself out from over the bed, having learned a severe lesson the night before. Soon he was floating around the room, corner to corner—turning, rolling, and moving up and down. He flew with his hands out in front of him, and down by his sides. He clasped them behind his neck. He put them under his chin, laughing at himself. Ling Wu was right. He'd never be lonely again. He could go anywhere.

Humming softly, Jon flew around his room for almost an hour and then guided himself back over the bed and gently lowered his body to the mattress. His brain did feel a bit tired from all the lifting, but not overly so. In fact, Jon felt quite good.

Smacks had given up watching the performances. As long as his master didn't crash, he was content to sleep.

Resting, Jon looked out the window and asked himself, *Do I dare?* There didn't seem to be much wind outside. Nothing like the nights when it attacked Clementine with howling force. It wasn't too chilly, either. He looked at the window for a long, long time and then nodded to himself.

Rise, Jon, he commanded silently, and came off the bed, taking a flight line for the open window. There were no mosquitoes or flies on Clementine, so none of the windows were screened. He went through as easily as a pigeon winging under an arch.

The night breeze flapped the legs of his pajamas and ruffled his hair as he circled over the grassy top of Clementine, keeping low at first, about four feet off the ground, then gaining altitude to ten. Jon couldn't help but grin wildly. He'd never felt so happy.

He rolled over on his back to look at the stars and then looked out across Three Fathom Shoal and Persiphone Reef, where white water broke over the rocks. *I'm the luckiest boy in the world,* he thought, and wished he could thank Ling Wu for this best of all gifts.

Clementine's light beam, sweeping around as usual, was too high to capture the pajama-clad figure as it did patterns over the grass and skimmed along the edges of the cliffs that plummeted to the jagged rocks and sea foam below.

Then Jon had an idea. *One brief flight around the top of the light.* He rose and rose and rose, and finally circled the lighthouse at 160 feet. The beam passed beneath him, then he went through it in a swan dive. He couldn't stop a laugh. If only his father and mother could see him. And Eunice Jones. They'd be speechless.

When he felt himself getting tired and cold, he glided down, slipping through the window as if all windows were made for small levitating boys.

Exhausted but happy, Jon Jeffers went to sleep, thinking about the next night, and the night after that, and the night after that. There was no reason at all not to put on warm clothing and take a float out over the ocean, see what was happening on old Persiphone, maybe even go the other direction, toward the lights of San Francisco.

~ TEN ~

OVER BREAKFAST THE NEXT MORNING, Jon's father asked, "No bad dreams last night, huh?"

Jon shook his head but found it difficult to look into his father's eyes. He felt guilty. He couldn't tell his parents about flying all over Clementine last night. He would never ever be able to tell them or anyone else. Keeping the secret was almost more than he could bear. Of course, dragon's bile and flaming straw in his nose would result if he didn't keep his word.

It was time to polish the lighthouse's windows and lenses. Even as high as the light tower was, salt spray, blown by the wind, coated the windows that protected the lenses in the old lantern room, so they had to be cleaned every second day. Using white toweling, Jon would rub the lower halves, his father the uppers.

About nine o'clock, they started up the winding ladder that ran through the lighthouse's interior for the first 140 feet, then around the exterior of the tower for the last twenty. It was on the exterior part that Jon first floated a few steps.

Bosun Jeffers, directly behind Jon, stopped. His laugh was puzzled. "I must be seeing things, Jon, but it looked like you just floated."

Jon felt panic. He hadn't intended to levitate. He hadn't directed his body to levitate.

"I kind of skipped," he replied. What had happened?

"On these steps, that's very dangerous."

"I won't do it again." Could his levitation get out of control? Ling Wu hadn't mentioned that possibility. And he certainly would have warned him.

Though maybe not.

Jon's father nodded, but his frown didn't go away. He shook his head. "That didn't look like a skip to me."

They went on up, and Jon reminded himself to be more careful in the future. But he hadn't been daydreaming as they climbed. The floating had surprised him as much as it had surprised his father. He was certain he hadn't told himself to float. Maybe his brain was having so much fun with levitation that it was taking control. That was a scary thought. He remembered Ling Wu cautioning him about something. What was it?

Perhaps he should try to contact Ling Wu and ask him what to do. He had no intention of stopping this wonderful, miraculous, sensational, extraordinary, supernatural use of his brain cells. But at the same time, he had to be able to control them.

THAT NIGHT, AT about ten-thirty, when the Jeffers were sleeping peacefully, Jon pulled on his jeans, a heavy wool shirt, and shoes. Then he put on his warmest jacket and his red wool cap. He said good-bye to Smacks and levitated several feet, straightened out, and passed through the window, crossing over the cove, heading for Persiphone Reef and Three Fathom Shoal.

Staying about thirty feet above the wave tops, he gazed about him and wondered how fast he was moving. Maybe ten miles an hour, maybe fifteen. The ocean was a mass of dark waves, broken here and there by patches of yellow silver as rollers crested. Now and then Jon could see trails of phosphorus as fish darted beneath the surface.

Most of his brain, almost all of it, was committed to levitation, but a few million stubborn cells lingered to worry about flight control. Was he his own pilot? His own navigator? But he soon pushed aside those uncomfortable questions and let the excitement of body flying, the pure joy of it, of being an eagle or a hawk, express itself with a shout: *"Wow!"*

It took just a few minutes to reach Persiphone, which was a long narrow shelf of coral a few thousand yards from Clementine, washed almost constantly by the ocean. He hovered a moment but saw nothing of interest. No ghosts down there.

Onward to Three Fathom Shoal, a quarter-mile north. Water boiled over the hidden, dangerous ledges capable of slicing a ship's bottom. Then he spotted a bobbing light farther out.

Positive it was a ship, Jon could not resist the temptation to investigate. It didn't seem too far away. But distances at sea, particularly at night, are often tricky, and the bobbing light was probably another mile west of the shoal.

Pressing on, watching as fish knifed below him, Jon was not aware that behind him the friendly light of Clementine was growing fainter. Nor was he aware that he was moving with a strong breeze.

Once, he almost collided with a gull that was beating its way south. Screeching angrily, the gull swerved off, a look of wide surprise in its eyes. Jon reminded himself to be more careful while navigating the night skies.

Closer, the bobbing light revealed a fishing boat with its nets out. Men were working on the lighted deck. Jon had never had an aerial view of a trawler and found it very interesting. In fact, it was so interesting that before he knew it, the strong breeze had carried him to within a few inches of the mast and, as he passed over the boat, had blown off his red cap.

"Good lord, what was that?" came a shout from the deck.

There were more shouts, and Jon knew he'd made a terrible mistake. Suddenly, a spotlight caught him. He saw the faces of a half dozen openmouthed fishermen as he skimmed into the dark on the opposite side of the boat. Ling Wu had said that people weren't accustomed to seeing other people levitate.

Isn't that the truth, Jon thought.

~ ELEVEN ~

JON MADE A WIDE CIRCLE AWAY FROM the boat and then headed back for Clementine, having learned that you just don't go about startling fishermen by floating across their mast in blue-black darkness.

Clementine Light was still strong but much farther away than Jon had thought. Suddenly, he realized the offshore wind that had helped push him to Persiphone and Three Fathom was now strong in his face, holding him back. He kept his nose straight into it and pushed on, knowing he'd be very weary by the time he reached the red cottage.

After an hour Clementine was still a half mile away, and Jon was nearly exhausted. He told his brain to add another two million cells to the job. As he gradually slipped from thirty feet down to ten, spray from the wave tops peppered his face. His hands felt almost frozen and his feet were numb. Every muscle and bone ached. He was wishing he'd never even *thought* about body flying.

Why, oh why, had he gone out so far? He thought of his warm, dry bed and his parents. If his brain cells suddenly failed, Jon would splash into the cold ocean and never be seen again. The breeze caught his tears and flung them behind him. With no one to hear, it wouldn't do any good to yell for help.

Near midnight Jon used his last ounce of energy to lift himself to the top of Clementine and glide down into the grass. He lay still for a moment, panting, but then finally got up and staggered toward the red cottage. He barely had the strength to climb into the window and crawl onto his bed.

Smacks almost wagged his tail off at the sight of his friend.

In the morning Jon's mother found him sprawled fully dressed on the yellow pelican spread, sleeping soundly. She left shaking her head.

～ TWELVE ～

JON WAS IN DEEP TROUBLE. OVER THE past three days, he'd levitated several times without calling on a single cell. There was no pattern to it, and he'd had to quickly anchor himself before his parents noticed. The only long-range solution to his problem was to again use telepathy to contact Ling Wu and beg for help.

The immediate problem was to stop his brain cells from acting on their own. He spent almost an hour thinking about it and then remembered reading an article in

Popular Science about deep-sea diving. Lead weights were used to pull divers down into the depths. So why not substitute small rocks for weights? Jon decided to try it.

Just before lunch Jon's father tapped him on the shoulder, and Jon suddenly came off the floor about two inches, the stones in his pants pockets rattling.

Perplexed once more, Bosun Jeffers asked, "How did you do that?"

"I just jumped," Jon said nervously, realizing he'd have to add a few more rocks as soon as possible. But people did jump when startled.

"That was a funny jump. I could swear you just went up into the air. Please do it again."

Jon's mother was looking on, frowning.

Hoping he wouldn't go up all the way to the ceiling and bump his head, Jon gave his toes a slight tap and rose six or seven inches.

"That's amazing!" his father exclaimed. "How did you learn to do that? I've never seen such a thing."

His mother said, "Jon, do you have gas in your stomach?"

Jon's face was as red as Ling Wu's gown. "It's easy. I just jump."

As they all sat down, Jon noticed that his parents were staring suspiciously at him. Worse, every time he moved, the stones rattled. Finally, his father looked all around the room for the source of the noise, and Jon confessed, "I picked up some rocks at the cove."

"Oh," his father said, clearing his throat and glancing at Jon's mother, a troubled look on his face. His mother's face mirrored the look. Did their nine-year-old son have a sudden physical problem of some kind? Jon was acting like he had a balloon inside him. Was it muscular? Something in his nervous system? Had a spirit invaded his body?

After lunch Jon got up very carefully. One thing was certain: He needed more anchoring weight. A few steps away from the door, probably because of all the bobbing stress and strain in the kitchen, Jon got the hiccoughs. Every time he went, "Eeglup," he rose several inches into the air.

Mrs. Jeffers called Bosun Jeffers over, and they watched in despair as their small son went across the green grass like a frog.

"Ee-glup." And hop.

"Ee-glup." And hop.

"Ee-glup." And hop.

Mrs. Jeffers said with determination, "Just as soon as that supply boat comes in, I'm taking him to the mainland and the hospital."

"Absolutely." Bosun Jeffers nodded.

Jon went back down to the cove and added three more stones to each pocket, then returned to the red cottage at the foot of the lighthouse and said he was going to take a nap. A long afternoon of emergency telepathy was ahead, to try to reach Ling Wu, a ghost Jon now wished he'd never met.

"That does it," Jon's mother said to Bosun Jeffers. "Jon hasn't volunteered to take a nap in five years."

As Jon walked out of the kitchen, a final massive hiccough grabbed him. He went, "Ee-glup," and his heels rose three inches despite the added stones.

Mrs. Jeffers began to weep.

Later that same day, there was some unusual excitement. A squadron of Army Air Corps fighter planes flew back and forth to the west of Clementine, about two miles out.

Rocks in his pockets, Jon went up the ladders to the top of the lighthouse and used his father's telescope to watch. The planes were Curtiss-Wright P-36s with Pratt and Whitney Twin Wasp engines. He wondered what they were doing.

THIRTEEN

THE NEXT DAY, WHILE UP ON THE TOWER platform, looking through the telescope at a tanker headed south, Jon spotted a small white boat moving toward Clementine. He focused in on it, and saw that it was Coast Guard, with three or four people aboard. Aside from when the steam supply-tug came, the only time an official boat visited the rock was for the annual lighthouse inspection.

There was chop, and the boat bounced through the whitecaps. Jon and Smacks quickly descended the ladders and steps. Jon's father was in the kitchen, busily making his monthly nonfood, maintenance needs list, which included oil for the diesel and other items.

"Dad, there's a Coast Guard boat approaching," said Jon. His father put down his pencil.

They went down to the cove, Smacks romping ahead, wagging his tail furiously. Visitors were always welcome.

The boat held three officers as well as a civilian and a two-sailor crew. The officers and civilian climbed out as the sailors tied the boat to the dock.

The Coast Guard lieutenant introduced himself and then the other two officers and the civilian. The major was from Army Intelligence, the lieutenant commander was from Naval Intelligence, and the civilian was an agent with the Federal Bureau of Investigation. Jon had never seen an agent, but he'd often listened to the FBI show on the radio. Now here was a real one.

Jon saw the frown and puzzled look on his dad's face. What in the world did these intelligence folks want on remote Clementine Rock? Jon felt the same way.

The lieutenant said, "Boats, could we have a chat?"

Jon's father said, "Sure. Let's go up to the kitchen. We'll have some coffee." He led the way, with Jon and Smacks following the group.

Jon wished he could talk to the FBI agent and ask him if he'd ever been in a gun battle with bootleggers.

They all sat down around the old oak

table while Mrs. Jeffers made coffee and asked if they wanted a piece of the apple pie she'd just baked. If the men turned it down, Jon thought, they were fools. Just breathing the smell of his mother's pies was a treat.

The lieutenant commander smiled at her and said, "Certainly. Thank you." He then said, "Tuesday night there was a trawler fishing about three quarters of a mile, perhaps a mile, off Three Fathom Shoal at approximately eleven o'clock. What I'm going to tell you now must remain top secret..."

Jon's mouth hung open and his heart did cartwheels.

"A flying object passed over this boat, circled it, and then disappeared into the darkness. Six of the eight crew members saw it, so it was not a figment of their imaginations. And it was not a big bird. You may laugh at what I will tell you next: The flying object was human and did not have wings or a motor."

Jon's legs began to turn to jelly.

"We all know it is impossible for humans to fly without wings or an engine. And if this flying object is indeed human, or a subhuman Martian, our country faces a complete security catastrophe."

Jon wanted to turn into a puddle on the floor.

"President Roosevelt is terribly worried, as are our military leaders. Beyond the possibility that someone has learned how to fly without wings or a motor, can you imagine millions of people, once the secret is out, flying all over the skies everywhere in the world? Can you imagine foreign flying soldiers, each carrying rifles and hand grenades?"

Jon wanted to run out and throw up on the grass, but he also wanted to keep listening.

"Wednesday morning the Army Air Corps sent out a squadron of fighters to search the area where the fishermen saw the flying object."

So that's what the planes were doing, Jon thought, feeling boneless. *Searching for me!* Should he tell them? Plead guilty? Promise never to levitate again? Suffer flaming straw up his nose?

"Now, my question to you, Boats, and to you, Mrs. Jeffers, and to you, sonny, is have you seen anything out here that might resemble an aerial vehicle, human or Martian?"

Bosun Jeffers shook his head. "Not me."

Mrs. Jeffers said, "My goodness, no."

Every eye on him, Jon had a millisecond decision to make. Boiled in dragon's bile or have his toes nailed to a shark's back? He said, "I was asleep *most* of Tuesday night," which was true, and the lieutenant commander let it go at that. Was he going to grill a four-foot-two, fifty-two-pound boy of nine? Jon never thought that a body-flight request to a living-dead magician would lead to this.

FOURTEEN

JON LISTENED INTENTLY AS THE ADULTS ate apple pie, drank coffee, and talked.

The FBI man said, "We have the fishermen in three suites at a San Francisco hotel with agents guarding the doors. The country could panic if news of this occurrence ever got out."

The army major said, "Whatever that was Tuesday night could be a scout for Martian invaders."

Jon wanted to say, "There are no Martian invaders; just me" but couldn't. He swallowed even though his mouth was desert dry.

The FBI agent said, "The only evidence we have is a red wool cap that landed on the trawler's deck. There's no label inside it. It was flown to Washington on Wednesday so our laboratory can analyze it. I personally don't think that Martians wear red wool caps."

Jon had never noticed there was no label inside that cap. What could the FBI tell from a label, anyway?

If he could keep himself from accidentally levitating until these men departed, he'd have a chance to think the whole unfortunate situation through and try again to contact Ling Wu, wherever he was, and stop the body flying forever. Never again would he body fly. Never. He'd gladly go back to being bored and lonely.

Not only was body flying against the laws of gravity, as his mother had said, it was apparently against the laws of the United States, and he could be put in jail for threatening the security of the entire nation. Did they have special jails for kids under twelve?

Before departing the lieutenant commander said, "Please keep a close watch on the skies and tell me immediately if you sight anything suspicious." He gave them the special command number for Operation Flying Object, headquartered in the White House.

Jon's father said, "I don't have a phone out here. I send emergency messages by Morse code."

The Coast Guard lieutenant said they'd handle that end and transfer any communications from Clementine to the intelligence chiefs and the president.

Under any other circumstances, Jon would have been fascinated with all the efforts to catch the so-called flying object. The situation went far beyond anything he'd ever read in *Popular Science*.

As he watched the boat pull away from the dock and head back to San Francisco, Jon wondered if he should now tell his parents that he'd learned to levitate from a living-dead Chinese magician. They'd already said they didn't believe in ghosts, and they'd probably take him to a mental hospital, where the levitation would only get worse. They'd have to strap him to a bed. What if the bed rose up? But he clearly remembered his oath never to tell that Ling Wu existed.

No, the best course of action was to make contact with the magician through telepathy and find out what was going wrong with his brain-cell signals. He couldn't very well live the rest of his life with rocks in his pockets or a diver's lead belt around his waist. Ling Wu would certainly understand.

So, Jon stayed down at the cove until lunchtime, sending message after message to Ling Wu, with no response. Perhaps the magician had finally died for good and would never visit the living world again. Perhaps he'd gone back to China.

After lunch Jon returned to the cove

and sat on the dory, exhausting himself by silently repeating, *Ling Wu, this is Jon Jeffers, come in, come in. Please, please! This is a life-and-death situation.*

After supper he pretended to be listening to the Grand Ole Opry with his parents, but he was actually performing telepathy. At bedtime he said a special prayer, asking God to help him locate Ling Wu. When he was certain his parents were both asleep, he dressed warmly and headed outside to spend the night in the cove. He'd read that radio waves lessened after nine o'clock, so maybe there'd be less interference with his telepathy.

As he was passing through the dark kitchen, he felt a surge of energy in his head and rose straight up. His skull lodged sideways against the ceiling, near the light fixture, and the rocks spilled out of his pockets onto the old oak table.

Smacks began to yelp.

Hearing all the ruckus, his parents rushed out of their bedroom, in their pajamas. They turned on the light and saw their only son flattened overhead like a butterfly, wearing warm clothes and a green wool hat.

~ FIFTEEN ~

BOSUN JEFFERS, WHO LOOKED LIKE HE'D just eaten a salamander, got a stepladder so he could pull Jon off the ceiling. The levitation was now so powerful that Jon didn't budge. "Did you put glue on yourself?" Bosun Jeffers asked.

Jon said, "No, Dad. I have a problem."

Jon's mother was speechless while his father wrestled him off the ceiling. She collapsed in a chair at the table.

When Bosun Jeffers finally got Jon down, he said, "Wedge your feet under

the table, son, so you don't go up again."
Then he went out to the maintenance shed
and came back with two buckets of mari-
time paint, called red lead, and told Jon
to put them in his lap. Together they
weighed what Jon weighed, with two
ounces to spare.

"Ballast, son," his father said. "Useful
for ships and levitating boys."

They all sat in silence, the reflection of
Clementine Light gliding through the
window on its regular cycle. Jon felt sick.

Finally, Bosun Jeffers spoke. "Jon, you
must tell us what has happened to you and
why. Your mother and I don't understand
what is going on here."

Despite the terrible threats from Ling
Wu, Jon knew he had to reveal every-

thing—except how he actually flew. *That* had to remain a secret.

It took almost two hours—with time out to make coffee and hot chocolate—for Jon to start back at the article on telepathy in *Popular Science* and bring the story up to Tuesday night when he flew over the *Cacciatore Roma*. Smacks had gone to sleep long before.

"So, it was *your* red cap that fell on the fishing boat," his mother said.

Jon nodded.

The part that the Jeffers found most difficult to believe involved the Chinese magician named Ling Wu, who had been dead since 1850.

They asked many questions about Ling Wu. It occurred to Mrs. Jeffers that Jon was the first human to fly without a motor, and she knew that many people, from the president on down—especially scientists and the FBI—would want to know a lot more about Ling Wu.

Jon said, "I've been trying to contact him. He's not responding. I may have to go through life weighted down. And if I lose my weights, I could go off into space."

"Oh no, oh no," his mother said, her eyes flooding with tears. "*Something* can be done. We'll go to a doctor tomorrow."

"What kind of doctor?" the bosun asked.

"I don't know. A specialist."

Jon thought about that. They'd have to find one who knew about levitation. That might be impossible.

Jon's mother, gazing at him sadly, asked, "How exactly do you fly?"

"I can't tell you. Ling Wu made me promise never to tell anyone."

"Son, you can tell us."

Jon shook his head. "Ling Wu threatened to stuff flaming straw up my nose and nail my feet to a shark's back."

"That's nonsense," the bosun said angrily. "Where can I find him?"

"I saw the shark, Daddy. I saw Ling Wu manufacture the straw. He's a magician and can do anything. He can even make me vanish."

Jon's father said tiredly, "Well, I have to send a message to those intelligence people. I don't know rightly what to say, except we aren't in danger of a Martian invasion."

Then he said, "Jon, please get me a pencil and tablet."

He sat for about a half hour, trying to write a message, tearing up page after page. Finally, he said, "You did all this, Jon. You should be the one to write it."

Jon nodded and began to write: *Mr. President, Martians aren't invading the U.S.A. Our son, nine-year-old Jon, learned how to levitate and flew over the trawler Tuesday night. Respectfully, Boatswain First Class James Jeffers and Mrs. Mabel Jeffers.*

The bosun read what Jon had written and said, "That's fine. I think you'll be answering a lot of questions."

He then went out to the lighthouse, climbed the steps and ladders and used the wireless set to dash-dot the words that would rock the civilized world: A nine-year-old boy could fly without a motor.

At last it was time for Jon to go to bed, but he knew he wouldn't get much sleep clinging to two buckets of red lead. So, his father held him down as Jon crawled between the covers, and his mother used all the safety pins she had to pin him between the sheets. He hoped he wouldn't need to get up during the night to use the john. If he did, that was just too bad.

∼ SIXTEEN ∼

BOSUN JEFFERS HAD TO STAY BEHIND
and to his duties as keeper of Clementine
Lighthouse, but Jon and his mother—and
Smacks, who was part of this whole af-
fair—were headed to San Francisco on the
same boat that had brought the intelligence officers to the rock.

This time there were security guards:
two sailors in the cabin with pistols on
their hips, and a sailor stationed on the
bow with a high-powered rifle. The nation couldn't afford to have Jon Jeffers
captured by Russian communists.

Jon, sitting in the cabin with his mother, the buckets of red lead by his side, felt as though he were going off to prison instead of to a hospital. Bosun Jeffers had sent another Morse code message during the night, requesting that the Coast Guard arrange medical attention.

He'd also received a message from his immediate lighthouse superiors—an insulting message asking him if he'd lost his mind and demanding a full report. The message said that the intelligence personnel involved were furious at the idea of his son claiming he could fly without a motor. Never in fourteen years of faithful service had Bosun Jeffers been subjected to such treatment, almost accused of treason.

The Coast Guard lieutenant, the army

major, the navy lieutenant commander, and the FBI agent were all waiting at the Coast Guard dock in San Francisco's Embarcadero when the boat arrived. Smacks jumped out first, wagging his tail as usual, then Mrs. Jeffers debarked.

The greeters stared at Jon, who was holding his red lead buckets. Their faces were unhappy—almost angry. Was this child playing tricks on them, making them look like fools?

The lieutenant commander said, in a hostile voice, "We've made arrangements for you to demonstrate your ability to fly without a motor." He looked at the buckets of primer, one in each of Jon's hands. "What are those?" he demanded.

"My anchors," Jon said. "Otherwise, I

could go up to the moon." He felt intimidated, even though it *was* nice to be in the city.

There was nasty laughter, and one angry-looking man said, "Ah, come on!"

You'll see, Jon thought.

"We can't do it out here on the docks, in case you can actually fly—which none of us believe—so I've arranged for the use of a high school gym."

Jon said, "You should also put a line around my ankle so I don't get caught up in the rafters."

The lieutenant commander looked at him as though Jon were as insane as Eunice Jones had predicted, then sighed. "All right."

They went off to the high school in

separate cars, the guards riding with Jon and his mother and Smacks. No one spoke. Jon felt like he was under arrest.

After they all filed into the school's gym, the armed guards took up position at the main door, securing the secrecy of the test. Even the janitor was sent out.

The Coast Guard lieutenant tied a three-eighths-inch yellow line to Jon's right ankle. There were fifty feet of it.

The FBI agent had brought along a photographer, who said, "This is one of the silliest things I've ever done."

Jon said, "Are you ready?"

"Yeah," said the naval officer.

The others repeated, "Yeah!"

Jon put his buckets of paint down and began to rise steadily.

The lieutenant commander said, "I'll be ——."

The major said, "I'll be ——."

The FBI agent said, "I'll be ——."

Jon began to fly around the gym as far and high as the rope would let him, smiling down at all of them.

The Coast Guard lieutenant applauded, and the others joined in.

For the fun of it, Jon made several aerial dives, and then called for the lieutenant to haul him back to the floor. The photographer took a picture of Jon with the FBI agent.

The agent, whose name was Hiram K. Forbes, said, "Just wait until the president hears about this." The lieutenant ran outside to call Letterman Hospital.

Agent Forbes said, "I demand to know how you do it."

"It's a secret," Jon said earnestly. "I cannot tell you."

"You'll have to tell the president."

Jon said, "No, sir, I won't."

The agent turned to Jon's mother. "Your son will be in a lot of trouble if he doesn't tell the president. He could be arrested under the reverse spy laws."

"Oh no, oh no," Mrs. Jeffers said, appearing faint.

"Oh yes," said Agent Forbes.

~ SEVENTEEN ~

THE BEST BRAIN SURGEON IN THE SAN Francisco area, if not in all of the United States of America, was Dr. Leon Buxtehede, a big-nosed hairy man of short stature who wore thick-lensed yellow plastic glasses. The hair on his head was as black as octopus ink, but his beard was pure white.

He had just finished listening to Jon's account of his meeting with Ling Wu, and the events thereafter, and was deep in thought. He'd asked Jon how he flew, and was exasperated when Jon refused to answer.

Meanwhile Jon was looking at a large color drawing of the human skull with words on it like *white matter* and *gray matter* and *medulla oblongata* and *cerebral peduncle*. His mouth sagged at the corners.

Dr. Buxtehede sat for a while longer gazing out over the famous Presidio, San Francisco's lovely military park. Finally, he said, "I could take X rays of your brain for the next week and consult with my colleagues all the way to Boston, but I really have no idea what to do."

Jon's hopes sank to the bottom of Three Fathom Shoal.

"This is the most unusual and difficult case I've ever encountered. I could open up your skull and try to find the answer, Mr. Jeffers. Clearly, the brain is involved, in my opinion."

You are totally right, Jon thought. *All the cells. Billions of them.*

Jon's mother said, "I feel faint."

Jon sincerely hoped his skull would not have to be opened. More than ever he wanted to talk to Ling Wu and end this business of having to carry buckets of paint around. He was past being weary of the red lead.

There was a knock on the door, and the FBI agent stuck his head in. "Mr. Jeffers, the president of the United States wants you to go to Washington, D.C., immediately. He wants to be the first person to be photographed with the boy who can fly without a motor."

Mr. Jeffers? Less than an hour before, Jon had been just a stupid kid who'd breached the security of the nation. Now the president wanted to meet him. Adults were strange. Jon said to Agent Forbes, "*You* were the first person to have your picture taken with me. You brought that photographer."

Agent Forbes said, "I'd appreciate it if you'd forget about that picture. Don't tell the president. Now, we must hurry. There's an aircraft fueling up."

Jon said, "What about my father? He'd like to meet the president."

The Coast Guard lieutenant said, "We don't have time to go out and get him. He'd have to be relieved. We'll fly him there tomorrow. This will be a breaking story all over the world."

Jon said, "I have to take my mother and Smacks."

Agent Forbes nodded and said to Dr. Buxtehede, "I'll bring your patient back in a few days."

The doctor was smiling widely. It wasn't every day he had a patient who would be photographed with the president. He said, "Be sure to mention my name to Mr. Roosevelt."

Then he said to Jon, "I'll be working night and day to find a way for you to keep on flying and at the same time have landing and takeoff control. I promise you, night and day!" He sprang up from behind his desk and shook Jon's hand and kissed a surprised Mabel Jeffers on the cheek. He even reached down to pat Smacks.

Off they went, with the usual guards

and even a motorcycle escort, to the airport.

Neither Jon nor his mother—or Smacks—had ever thought they'd fly in an airplane. But then again Jon never thought he'd fly, period. Soon they were cruising east at ten thousand feet in a navy twin-engined DC-3.

As they crossed the Grand Canyon, the plane bouncing all over the sky, Jon realized he could never again call himself the loneliest boy on Earth. He was about to be known from Washington to Tibet.

Bucking strong headwinds, the DC-3 had to be refueled twice before it landed at Anacostia Naval Air Station at about 4:00 A.M. Agent Forbes said, "I'll bet you sleep in the Lincoln bedroom the rest of the night." Jon had heard of Abraham Lincoln but not his bedroom in the White House.

"And you'll probably have breakfast with the president and first lady in the morning."

"Will you be there?"

"I doubt it very much. If anybody discovers I was photographed with you, I'll be assigned to Arkansas."

Jon had begun to like Hiram K. Forbes, and he said, "I'll keep our secret, but I won't tell the president how I fly."

The agent sighed and thanked him and shook his hand as White House people rushed to the DC-3 stairway to greet the first human to fly without a motor.

Agent Forbes said that Secret Service agents would be taking care of him as long as he was in Washington. Jon had read about them in *Popular Science*. They followed the president everywhere he went. They even watched the chefs cooking his food before the president could take a bite.

Two stern-faced Secret Service agents got into the limousine with them, and Jon noticed two other black cars, one ahead and one behind, loaded with men in black suits. *Even a Martian might not get better protection,* Jon thought.

Soon Mrs. Jeffers, Jon, and Smacks arrived at the White House and were offered a snack before being shown to the Lincoln bedroom. Mrs. Jeffers said, "Never in my life did I think this Nebraska girl would sleep where the Lincolns slept."

There was a temporary crisis when she

asked a maid for all the safety pins in the White House.

It had been another exhausting day for Smacks, and he jumped into the bed between Jon and his mother, perhaps the first four-legged creature ever to nestle down on the fancy spread under which Abe and Mary Todd had spent their nights.

Jon thought the mattress was hard. Maybe it was the original one?

~ EIGHTEEN ~

JON HAD SEEN PHOTOS OF PRESIDENT and Mrs. Roosevelt in the *Chronicle* and had listened on Sunday nights to his famous "fireside chats" on the Jeffers's new Philco radio set. The family listened to his program so regularly, it was like going to church.

He'd also seen President Roosevelt in the newsreels at the picture shows on the mainland whenever his parents took him. The president had a nice smile and wore rimless glasses. He seemed to care for all Americans.

Jon hadn't seen or heard Mrs. Roosevelt much, but she seemed nice, too. He remembered seeing her in the Fox Movietone News, touring a poor section of the country called Appalachia. His mother had said, "She's a different first lady; nothing fancy about her. Look at that plain dress and that little hat."

And now here he was at the White House, soon to meet Franklin and Eleanor Roosevelt.

AT BREAKFAST, JON told of his adventures flying over the lighthouse and the *Cacciatore Roma,* and how it all started with the Chinese magician, but not how he actually flew. He thought Ling Wu might forgive him for everything except betraying the secret of levitation. Telling that would bring on the flaming straw and the shark.

Along with the president and the first lady, the admirals commanding the navy and the Coast Guard—as well as the generals commanding the army and the Army Air Corps—attended the breakfast. These were the men in charge of defending the United States of America, and people flying around without motors were a definite threat to the country's well-being.

The man in charge of the FBI was also there. He had a face like a bulldog and a body like a warthog, just as compact. His name was Hoover.

The president explained Jon's buckets to those at the table by saying there was some type of temporary imbalance with Jon's system, but one of the world's foremost neurosurgeons, Dr. Leon Buxtehede, had assured him a solution was soon to be found. Jon would by no means have to carry gallons of red lead around the rest of his life. Everyone nodded solemnly.

Jon and his mother sat opposite President Roosevelt and the first lady. Smacks was beneath the table, having been fed in the kitchen. Everyone was as nice to Smacks as they were to Jon and his mother.

The president said, "Now, Jon, you have to tell us how you do it."

"I'm sorry, sir, but I can't. I took an oath never to reveal that secret."

"Come now, Jon, your secret is safe in this room," said the president.

The navy admiral insisted, "Tell us."

"Yes," said the army general.

The FBI man named Hoover ordered, "Boy, tell us. Or else."

Mrs. Roosevelt interrupted. "Stop it, Franklin—all of you. Jon is only nine."

"All right, Eleanor, we'll discuss it later," the president said.

Then he smiled at Jon. "I can't wait to see you fly."

"Neither can I," said Mrs. Roosevelt.

The admirals and generals and Mr. Hoover took their cue, and all agreed that they, too, couldn't wait.

"The whole world is waiting, Jon. More than two hundred newspaper reporters and radio reporters and photographers will be on the lawn at ten-thirty to see you fly without a motor. The movie newsreel people will be there, too. You'll be on the screens of every movie theater in the country within three days, then overseas," said the president.

The Coast Guard admiral said, "It boggles my mind to think that one of our Coast Guard children achieved this unbelievable feat."

It wasn't until that moment that Jon considered the possibility that his aerial brain cells might not be working this morning or might even refuse to cooperate. He began to get very nervous.

The first lady said, "Well, now that breakfast is over, I'll take you on a tour of our house, so my husband can get a little work done before your historic moment."

Jon, his mother, and Smacks followed her into rooms that would never be seen by the average citizen. Jon's mother whispered into his ear, "Tell the president in private how you fly."

The buckets banging against his knees, he whispered back, "I can't." How would *she* feel, nailed to the back of a shark?

The tour ended in the Oval Office, where the president did his hardest work and made decisions that affected the entire world. FDR smiled and said, "Jon, now will you tell me how you do it?"

Jon panicked, blurting, "I have to go to the bathroom," clearly the dumbest answer ever given to any chief executive of the United States of America.

Mr. Hoover followed Jon into the

bathroom and grabbed him by his left ear, growling, "You better tell the president how you do it, or I'll throw you in jail for as long as you live."

"Owww!" Jon yelled.

Just then the Coast Guard admiral entered and said loudly, "What are you doing, J. Edgar?"

Mr. Hoover scowled at the Coast Guard admiral. "Russian communist agents could kidnap him."

"Hardly," the Coast Guard admiral said. "I'll have a boat patrolling the lighthouse day and night."

~ NINETEEN ~

THE PRESS HAD BEEN GATHERING ON THE lawn since eight o'clock. At last count there were more than three hundred people, including correspondents from around the globe. Chairs to accommodate the president, the first lady, Jon's mother, and Jon himself faced the batteries of cameras, microphones, and print reporters. A White House aide held Smacks's leash.

The president introduced Jon and Mrs. Jeffers, even Smacks.

As quickly as he could, Jon told the story of Ling Wu for the sixth or seventh time. He then answered questions—but not about how he flew—for a good fifteen minutes, until President Roosevelt's press secretary stepped forward and told Jon to proceed with the demonstration.

Holding the buckets, Jon waited until the press secretary tied one end of a fifty-foot yellow line to his ankle, the other end to an anvil. There was such a hush over the audience that only the sound of cawing crows could be heard. The press secretary whispered, "That anvil will be a museum piece someday."

Jon closed his eyes and called upon five hundred million cells to lift his feet off the ground. He dropped the ballast buckets and shot up into the air like a rocket to *oooooohs* and *ahhhhs* from the audience, and then thunderous applause.

He flew around the lawn at the end of his tether and was photographed with the president and the first lady. Although a war had recently begun in Europe, Jonathan Jeffers captured headlines around the world the next day.

Jon and his mother, who had now been joined by Bosun Jeffers, stayed on in Washington for another six days of sight-seeing. Several shoemakers offered to provide Jon with lead-soled shoes, but he decided that twenty-five pounds of lead on each foot would become very tiresome, especially since he only weighed fifty-two pounds. Jon decided to keep carrying the buckets for the time being, until Dr. Buxtehede could come up with a solution. And anyway, he liked the shoulder muscles he was developing.

When the Jeffers returned to San Francisco, hundreds of people were there to greet them, including the press and Hiram K. Forbes. He hadn't been reassigned to Arkansas, after all. The photo of him and Jon had remained a secret and was now in a safety deposit drawer at the main branch of the Bank of America, hidden from the eyes of White House busybodies.

There was a hurriedly assembled parade. The Jeffers sat in the back of a long open Cadillac, waving to the crowds along Market Street, just like Lindbergh had done eight years earlier. There was a reception in the mayor's office, and Jon received the key to the city. The Coast Guard Command saluted him with a luncheon. There was a huge dinner at the

Mark Hopkins Hotel, with every notable in town attending, including Dr. Buxtehede, who whispered to Jon, "Come see me tomorrow."

The next day, Dr. Buxtehede was waiting for Jon and his parents in his office. He put on a brave smile when they entered, shook hands all around, and then admitted, that despite twenty-hour days and endless conversations with his colleagues all the way to Boston and across to London, he'd had no success.

Mrs. Jeffers said, "Oh no, oh no."

"However, there is one last hope before I have to open your skull, Jon. Two nights ago I spent an evening backstage at the Pagoda Theater with a very old Chinese magician named Shue Ming, which in English means 'speak bright.' He knew all about Ling Wu but not how to contact him."

Mrs. Jeffers said, with deep frustration, "Where *is* that man?"

Dr. Buxtehede continued, "I took notes. Shue Ming believes there is a cure for what you have, Jon, that dates back five thousand years. He said you will have to swallow a mixture of scales from the Purple Carp, dust from the paws of the Horrible Bear, and a tear from the Great Idol of Kokmong."

Aghast, Mrs. Jeffers asked, "Fish scales?"

Bosun Jeffers asked, "Where are these things? We'll get them."

Dr. Buxtehede held up a hand. "Wait!" He consulted his notes. "Two thousand years ago the sacred Purple Carp was removed from the Forbidden City pool because of threats that heathens would steal it."

There's that word again, Jon thought.

"It is now believed to be in the cold depths of Sun Moon Lake, at the foot of the Thangla mountains, in Tibet."

"And the Horrible Bear?" Jon asked.

"He is in a mountain cave not far from Sun Moon Lake."

"And the Great Idol of Kokmong?"

Dr. Buxtehede took off his glasses. He had very warm brown eyes, like Jon's. "He is closer, in the South China Sea. On the island of Kokmong, of course."

"How will we get the Purple Carp scales, the bear dust, and the tear from that Kokmong idol once we get there?" Mr. Jeffers asked.

"Shue Ming said that only Ling Wu can obtain them," said the doctor.

Jon's hopes vanished. He'd let the whole world know that Ling Wu existed. He had broken all the oaths except one. He deserved every terrible punishment that Ling Wu had threatened to use. The only thing he could do, if he could even summon the magician from wherever he was, was to ask Ling Wu to have mercy on him, the nine-year-old heathen who had the brains of an ant.

"Thank you for all your help," he said to Dr. Buxtehede.

The kindly neurosurgeon replied, "I hope you find him."

"So do I," said Jon, with thoughts of carrying red-lead buckets or wearing lead-soled shoes as long as he lived filling his mind.

After five days in San Francisco, the heavyhearted and sad-faced Jeffers, and Smacks, went to the Coast Guard landing and boarded the steam tug for the trip back to Clementine Lighthouse.

There was a big bag of mail waiting on the tug. Every living relative of the Jeffers had written, some asking if they could come and spend time at the lighthouse. The bosun shouted, "Are they all crazy? Our table only sits four!"

There were hundreds of letters to Jon. Everyone wanted to know how to body fly. There was even a letter from Eunice Jones: *You're famous! Just to think you're sleeping in my old room! You must have had help from those ghosts. I've got to talk to you.*

~ TWENTY ~

ON THE WAY BACK, THE BOAT GENTLY rising on the sparkling, cold blue sea, the Jeffers talked about Jon's problem.

His mother said, uncomfortably, "Son, we know about your imagination—how big it is. Did you, did you..." She stopped and took a breath. "Did you invent Ling Wu and somehow teach yourself to fly?"

Bosun Jeffers, with a grave face, tried to finish her thought. "Not being natural for humans, it somehow..."

Jon shook his head. "Ling Wu is real, believe me."

The Jeffers fell silent. Feeling defeated, they stared down at the deck. Their only son was ill physically—and maybe mentally, too.

Before too long, the tug arrived at the dock. Wishing that it would steam on past Clementine, steam on forever, and not return him to his old lonely life, Jon untied the rope that attached him to his seat, picked up his buckets once again, and followed Smacks's leap to the dock.

The memories of the night flight over the *Cacciatore Roma,* Hiram K. Forbes and the Roosevelts, the White House lawn, and Dr. Buxtehede were still very fresh in Jon's mind.

FOR THE NEXT thirty-two days Jon trudged up and down the fifty-four steps to Clementine's cove, carrying the buckets of red lead, and trying to summon Ling Wu. He thought the isolated cove might help his telepathy signals reach the great magician.

He also climbed the 155 inner and outer lighthouse steps to the platform, resting at every 10 steps. Perhaps Ling Wu would hear him from up there.

But tears usually flowed before he reached the top. The buckets seemed to weigh fifty pounds each. The bosun had wrapped padding around the wire handles, but Jon had worn creases in his palms and now wore leather gloves. He'd lost ten pounds, which he could ill afford.

The bosun volunteered to strap his son on his back, carry him to the cove, and secure him with a rope near the dory rock.

He even offered to do the same up on the lantern platform.

But Jon decided both plans were risky. If Ling Wu saw his father en route to either mental-message-sending location, the magician might forgo his visit.

Using telepathy, Jon pleaded every day with Ling Wu to return to the cove rock or the lighthouse or any other place on which the magician might choose to alight. Meanwhile the Coast Guard boat circled the cove around the clock to keep the Russians from kidnapping Jon. During the day his father also kept watch with his telescope.

At last, on the thirty-third day, Jon discovered Ling Wu sitting at the exact same spot on the rock beside the dory where Jon had first met him. His skin was red with anger. He'd changed clothing. His gown was now a shining green; his pants were coal black; his shoes were silver-colored, as was the tiny hat on his head.

He said, "You miserable heathen, you tick on a cow's back—"

"Where have you been, Ling Wu? I've been trying to call you for more than a month."

"None of your insignificant business where I've been."

"I'm in deep trouble, Ling Wu."

"I know you are. You didn't listen. I knew you wouldn't listen. You upset your brain cells flying back from that fishing boat without practice. I warned you to be careful."

"I apologize."

"That's not enough. Not only did you not listen, you broke your vow. Are you ready for dragon's bile and flaming straw and the shark's back?"

"Please, don't do that to me!" cried Jon in alarm. "Please forgive me, Ling Wu. I made mistakes. Don't boil me in dragon's bile. Don't sentence me to a lifetime of carrying weights around so I don't go to the moon. I plead guilty. I was lonely. The whole world was passing me by. I had no friends except Smacks. I felt trapped on this rock."

Ling Wu looked west, toward the horizon.

"Have you ever been lonely, Ling Wu, really lonely?"

The magician looked north, toward San Francisco. Then he looked up, with his silly spyglass, at the lighthouse, at Jon's father. "Hmh."

"Please, Ling Wu. There's an old magician in Chinatown who said he knows the five-thousand-year-old cure."

"Shue Ming?" Ling Wu asked scornfully.

Jon nodded.

"He knows nothing! The best of Shue Ming is turning kerchiefs into doves."

Jon wasn't interested in Shue Ming's best, nor was he interested in Dr. Buxtehede opening his skull to adjust his misbehaving brain cells. "Please, please, O great, great magician, I'll never fly again, I—"

Ling Wu's eyes, which matched the

green of his gown, bored into Jon's soul. "This is not about flying, insignificant beetle. It is about your word to me, which you have broken. Repeat after me: I, Jon Jeffers, will never again speak the name of Ling Wu. I will honor my bond of silence."

Jon held up his right hand, as if being sworn in at the Celestial Court. In a voice as clear as a trumpet, righteous as a psalm, truthful as the Three Kneelings and Nine Knockings, Jon repeated each word: "'I, Jon Jeffers, will never again speak the name of Ling Wu. I will honor my bond of silence.'"

Ling Wu nodded.

Jon waited, then said, "Is that all? Can I stop levitating now?"

"No, miserable ant, you cannot stop levitating now. You must think before you can do that."

"Think of what?"

"Think of what I have told you."

Desperately, Jon thought back over all Ling Wu had said to him when they first met. Words about soaring, about levitation, about hawks and hummingbirds, about—

"Kites!" cried Jon.

"Now, unworthy, you begin to use your brain," said Ling Wu.

"But what do I do now?" begged Jon.

"What does a kite have that you do not?" replied Ling Wu.

"A string!"

Ling Wu looked to the east. "And what is your string, miserable frog?"

Jon thought, thought harder than he ever had before—harder, even, than when he had learned to levitate. What held him to Earth the way a string holds a kite?

The answer was easy: It was his family, of course.

He concentrated still harder—so hard, he heard clickings and grindings and squeakings inside his brain, then finally a few bars of serene music.

"Close your eyes, heathen ant," Ling Wu said. "Good-bye, forever."

Jon did as directed and heard temple bells. After a few seconds he opened his eyes and looked around. Ling Wu was gone. Jon looked west. A sliver of green gossamer cloud was vanishing high in the sky.

"Thank you and good-bye," Jon called out softly.

He dropped the paint buckets, needing them no longer, and shouted for Smacks, who scampered down the fifty-four steps, then scampered back up, barking louder than ever.

Jon, his feet on the ground, his heart firmly tied to the earth, followed his best friend home.

Another acclaimed story by Theodore Taylor

The Maldonado Miracle

~

A small town gets a big miracle.

TWELVE-YEAR-OLD JOSE MALDONADO USED TO dream of becoming a fine artist. But this son of a poor Mexican farmer now focuses on survival, not art. After Jose's mother died, his father left to work in the United States, leaving Jose on his own in Mexico. When it's time for father and son to reunite, things go terribly wrong. Jose's attempt to cross the border is harrowing, and his stay at a migrant worker camp turns into a nightmare, forcing him to flee for his life. Hiding out in a church seems a wise thing to do, until the blood dripping from Jose's wounded shoulder lands on a statue of Christ. Now everyone thinks the statue itself is bleeding. Jose's accidental "miracle" kick-starts a media frenzy—and threatens the future of an entire town.

Theodore Taylor's uncompromising look at the power of love, hope, and redemption inspired the Showtime movie *The Maldonado Miracle,* which garnered major critical acclaim at the Sundance Film Festival.

Also look for Theodore Taylor's forthcoming

ICE DRIFT

A chilling survival story

THE YEAR IS 1868, AND FOURTEEN-YEAR-OLD ALIKA and his younger brother, Sulu, are hunting for seals on an ice floe attached to their island in the Arctic Ocean. Suddenly the ice starts to shake, and they hear a loud crack—the terrible sound of the floe breaking free from land! The boys watch with horror as the dark expanse of water between the ice and the shore rapidly widens and they start drifting south—away from their home, their family, and everything they've ever known.

Throughout their six-month-long icebound journey down the Greenland Strait, the brothers face bitter cold, starvation, and most frightening of all, vicious polar bears. Their thrilling story of adventure and survival is a moving testament to the bond between brothers—and to the strength of the human spirit.